Jane Hissey

Li   s

Please renew/return items by last date
shown. Please call the number below:

Renewals and enquiries: 0300 1234049

Textphone for hearing or
speech impaired users: 01992 555506

www.hertfordshire.gov.uk/libraries
L32

Hertfordshire

THE sun shone through the window and woke Little Bear. 'What a lovely morning,' he said to himself. 'I'll do something different today.'

HE took off his pyjamas and looked for his trousers.
He looked on the chair where he'd left them. Then he
looked under the bed. Then he looked in the chest of
drawers in case they were there. But they weren't.
They were nowhere.

'Trousers can't disappear,' cried Little Bear. 'I'll see if
Old Bear has seen them.'

OLD Bear was enjoying the sun in his deckchair when Little Bear found him.

'Hmm . . . trousers,' he said. 'I haven't seen them, I'm afraid, but Camel was here just now. Perhaps she knows where they are.'

LITTLE Bear soon found Camel. 'I did find them,' she said. 'I was feeling cold and I thought they were a pair of hump warmers. These are better, though,' she added, showing Little Bear two bobble hats: one for each hump. 'They are much warmer.'

'Can I have my trousers back, then?' asked Little Bear.

'Oh, sorry Little Bear, I didn't know they were yours. I gave them to Sailor to use as sails for his boat. Come on, I'll take you there.'

But when they found Sailor he had white sails on his boat.

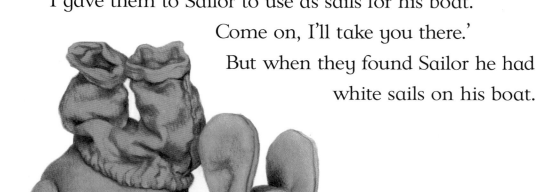

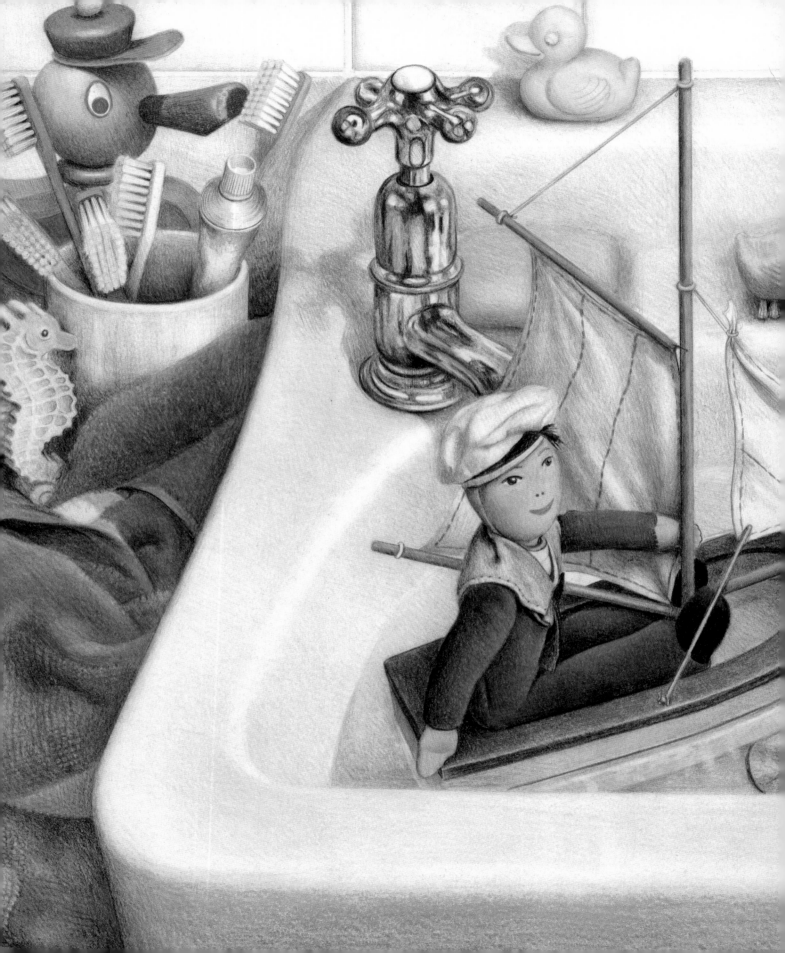

'THE sails Duck gave me looked too much like trousers,' he explained.

'That's because they *are* trousers,' said Little Bear. 'Where are they now?'

'I gave them to Dog to keep his bones in,' said Sailor. 'Sorry, Little Bear. You'd better hurry and find him.'

Dog was burying his bones in flowerpots when Little Bear found him.

'They kept falling through the two-bone bone-holder,' he explained.

'TWO-BONE BONE-HOLDER!' cried Little Bear. 'Those were my trousers!'

'Oh, dear,' said Dog. 'I gave them to Rabbit to use as a skiing hat. I am sorry, Little Bear.'

'WHEEE!' cried Rabbit, as he shot past Little Bear, skiing down the bannister on two lolly-stick skis. But there were no trousers on his head.

'I did have them,' he explained when Little Bear caught up with him. 'They made a lovely hat with lots of room for my ears. Then they slipped over my eyes and I crashed so I gave them to Zebra. She was building herself a house.'

ZEBRA had finished her house when Little Bear arrived. But his trousers were nowhere to be seen.

'I did use them,' she said. 'I put them on my back and carried all these bricks in them.'

'What happened to them then?' asked Little Bear.

'I gave them to Duck to use as a flag for his sandcastle. Sorry, Little Bear. I didn't know you'd lost them.'

D UCK was in the sand tray making sandcastles. He had a paper flag to put on the top.

'Zebra gave me a lovely flag,' he sighed. 'But Bramwell borrowed it to use in the kitchen.'

'Was it red?' asked Little Bear.

'Bright red,' said Duck.

'And did it look like trousers?'

'Hmm,' said Duck, 'I suppose it did.'

'Those were my trousers,' said Little Bear, 'and I really need them back.'

They hurried to the kitchen where they found bowls and spoons and eggs and flour, and in the middle of it all sat Bramwell Brown.

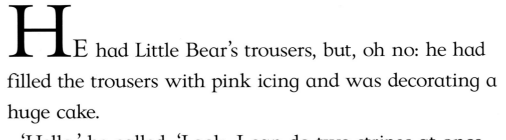

HE had Little Bear's trousers, but, oh no: he had filled the trousers with pink icing and was decorating a huge cake.

'Hello,' he called. 'Look, I can do two stripes at once with these icing bags!'

'But they're not icing bags; they're my trousers!' cried Little Bear.

'Oh dear,' said Bramwell Brown. 'I thought I'd seen them before.'

'DON'T worry,' said Old Bear. 'The icing will wash out and they'll be as good as new.'

'I hope so,' said Little Bear. 'I don't want them all sticky. Who is the cake for?'

'It's for all of you,' said Bramwell Brown.

'A Trousers Day cake!' laughed Old Bear.
And that's what Bramwell wrote on the cake.

It said 'Happy Trousers Day' in the middle and there was a trousers pattern round the edge.

DUCK washed Little Bear's trousers and dried them next to the cooker. Then all the toys sat down to enjoy a piece of cake and to celebrate the day Little Bear lost, and found, his trousers.

AND ever since Trousers Day, Little Bear has slept with his trousers under his pillow.

'Nobody will find them there!' he says.

For my mother · in her memory

SALARIYA

www.salariya.com

This edition published in Great Britain in MMXIII by Scribblers, a division of Book House,
an imprint of The Salariya Book Company Ltd
25 Marlborough Place,
Brighton BN1 1UB

www.scribblersbooks.com
www.janehissey.co.uk

First published in Great Britain in MCMLXXXVII by Hutchinson Children's Books

ISBN-13: 978-1-908177-83-4

3 5 7 9 8 6 4 2

A CIP catalogue record for this book is available from the British Library.

Printed and bound in China
Printed on paper from sustainable sources
Reprinted in MMXIII